DISCOVER SERIES
PETS

MASCOTAS

Gato

Cat

Chinchilla

Chinchilla

Perro

Dog

Rana

Frog

Pez de Colores

Goldfish

Pinzón de Gould

Gouldian Finch

Conejillo de Indias

Guinea Pig

Hámster

Hamster

Cangrejo Ermitaño

Hermit Crab

Caballo

Horse

Ratoncito de Casa

House Mouse

Gatito

Kitten

Lagartija

Lizard

Ratoncito

Mouse

Tritón

Newt

Perico

Parakeet

Loro

Parrot

Poni

Pony

Cachorro

Puppy

Conejo

Rabbit

Ratón

Rat

Serpiente

Snake

Tortuga

Tortoise

Tortuga

Turtle

Make Sure to Check Out the Other Discover Series Books from Xist Publishing:

Published in the United States by Xist Publishing
www.xistpublishing.com
PO Box 61593 Irvine, CA 92602

© 2018 by Xist Publishing All rights reserved
Translated by Victor Santana
No portion of this book may be reproduced without express permission of the publisher
All images licensed from Fotolia
First Bilingual Edition

ISBN: 978-1-5324-0679-9   eISBN: 978-1-5324-0680-5

xist Publishing

www.ingramcontent.com/pod-product-compliance
Lightning Source LLC
LaVergne TN
LVHW070950070426
835507LV00030B/3482